The Christmas *Breakdown*

LISAMARIE KADE

ONE

I brushed my chestnut colored hair out of my face for what felt like the twentieth time in the past five minutes.

The wind that came off the Florida Coast was brutal. Even though it was mid December, it was still warm and sticky. Yet, there I sat, contemplating my life.

I had just ended my relationship with Tanner the day after Thanksgiving. I was over it. He really had no plans to grow up. Not any time soon anyway. I, on the other hand, was ready to purchase a home and settle into life. One I used to picture sharing with Tanner. Unfortunately, video games and wanting to party and get drunk was still a priority to him. Twenty six years old and still acts like a frat boy.

It was a bitter pill to swallow, wasting over three years of my life with him. But, I'm looking forward to getting the hell out of this beach town for the holiday. We had planned to visit his family in South Florida, but now I'm free and can do what I want to do. The only downfall is that my family already planned a trip away to Canada and there was no possible way I could pull that off in just a few short weeks.

Instead, I'll be going to my cousin, Jessy's cabin, where I'll retreat for a few weeks. She's a workaholic who isn't joining in on the family trip. It'll be nice though, because she will be so busy with work that I'll practically have the place to myself.

I allowed the sun to beat down on my face for just a few more minutes before packing up my belongings to head home. I needed a shower and to pack so I could hit the road first thing in the morning with no looking back.

TWO

With my small blue SUV packed and ready to go, I hit the road before the sun came up. It's a seven hour drive to Jessy's cabin in the mountains of Georgia. Truth be told, I wouldn't have cared if it was a twelve hour drive. I need a change of scenery and her mountainside cabin is the cure.

About three hours into my drive, Jessy sent a text that said weather was coming. What kind of weather? She didn't specify. Rain, snow? I have no idea. Hoping it's rain because I've never driven in snow. Actually, I have only experienced snow once and that was on a Christmas vacation when I was about ten.

Okay, so maybe this spontaneous trip during the winter wasn't the brightest idea. It was all I had to work with though. I don't want to text her back while driving so my fingers are crossed for rain. I'll call when I get closer to her place.

Helen, Georgia was still about an hour away. I sighed as I got off the highway to stop for gas. My legs and back ache from sitting for so long. Almost there I told myself. Almost there.

After pumping gas and getting a Reese-cup to hold me over, I went to start my SUV. It took two tries to get it to crank over and that now has me a little concerned. My car is a few years old but it has never given me trouble. Shaking it off, I head back out on the road.

After getting off the highway, I pull up to a fork in the road and bam! My engine shuts off.

I try turning the key over several times, but no luck.

Fuck my life.

There's nothing around me either. Literally just a bunch of fields and no damn cell phone service. I've tried my cousin a few times now and the call keeps dropping.

I try to calm the growing frustration, or maybe it's panic, I can't be sure. I'm in a town I don't know, with my car not starting.

I decide to put the window down to breathe

in some fresh air. Thank goodness for a base model and crank windows. Fresh air will help.

What do I do now?

As if on cue, an old beat up white pickup pulls up next to me. I can smell the exhaust as the truck stops at the stop sign. Gross, yet that's not all. Christmas music blasts from the truck and the driver, a guy has a Santa beard and a Santa hat on. Sans shirt.

What on earth?

The guy, whose eyes are bright blue, nods his head once and takes a left. There I am left baffled by the shirtless Santa that just drove past.

Is this how they do things up here?

THREE

I sent Jessy a text, hoping that somehow, someway, the cell towers pick up my signal and graciously deliver my text. There's nothing quite like holding a cell phone out of my window up high in an attempt to gain service. Also, I hope she knows the crossroads that I'm currently stuck at.

A light rain has started and I don't know if I should be relieved or worried. Does it rain before it snows? Or is it just a little rain storm? These are things I probably should have researched before jumping in my car to head up here.

You dummy, Tamera. This is what happens when you fly by the seat of your pants. All I was thinking about was running away and—

Is that the white truck that just passed by a few minutes ago?

Sure enough, shirtless Santa is pulling up to the stop sign, except instead of going on his merry way (like what I did there), he pulls over slightly and hops out of his truck.

Holy hell. Shirtless Santa has abs that go on for days, all the way down they go, disappearing below his denim shorts.

"Ma'am?"

Oh shit, he said something. I did hear, except I wasn't listening. I was too busy ogling his stomach.

"I'm sorry, I missed what you said."

"I noticed." Those blue eyes wink once. "Do you need any help?" A smirk splayed across his face that not even his fake, white beard could hide.

Crap, he caught me checking him out.

"Um, I don't think so. My car broke down and I am having signal trouble. Well, maybe if I could just borrow your phone to call my cousin." And there I go, rambling like a damn fool. Get it together girl. He's just a guy, like all the rest of them. Immature and hot. Very hot.

"Mind if I check under the hood?" He asks as he hands me his cell phone.

With a shake of my head, I pop the hood and try to call Jessy.

It rings a few times before she finally picks

up, probably because she doesn't know this number that I am calling from.

"Hello?"

"Hey, it's Tamera, um—"

"Hey! Are you close?"

"Actually, I'm broke down, not too far from town, I think."

"Oh no. There's a storm coming, let me see if I can locate a tow company. I'll call you right back."

She hangs up before I can tell her I have no service. Great.

Shirtless Santa peaks from out under the hood. "Give it a crank."

I do and nothing happens. Nothing at all.

This dude probably knows nothing about cars either.

I hop out, hoping he's not gonna try to kidnap me.

"My cousin lives in Helen, she's gonna try to find me a tow, but thanks for trying."

The guy looks me up and down from head to toe, completely assessing me. I know he ain't checking me out. My brown curls are thrown up in a messy bun, zero makeup, and I'm in a pair of sweats paired with a band tee that's seen better days.

"There's a nasty storm that's about to hit, you

might want to ride into town and bunk at my place until it passes."

What? No way.

"Um, yeah no thanks. I mean, I don't even know you. You could be like a mass murderer."

I turn to head back to my SUV. First thing I plan to do once inside is lock the doors.

"I could be or I could be a gentleman who doesn't want to leave some chick who clearly isn't from here stranded."

I stop in my tracks. His words are bitter rolling off his tongue and for a second I feel a little guilty for accusing him of being a murderer.

"I'm sorry, it's just.... look, I don't know you. I don't know this town and it's probably best I just hang tight until the tow company arrives."

"Which company is your cousin, you said, using?"

I bite my lip, she didn't tell me because she was looking for a company.

"What's your name?" He asks.

"Tamera." Why I decide to tell him is beyond me. This crazy Santa impersonator could seriously kidnap me and leave me for dead in these fields.

"Aren't you gonna ask my name? Or do you not want to know the name of your could be killer?"

Great. Now I feel super bad and slightly stupid.

"I'm sorry. I shouldn't have accused you. What is your name?"

"Wesley, but everyone calls me Wes."

That's a nice name. A nice name that goes with that nice body and those nice eyes. Speaking of, those piercing blue eyes are staring at me.

"Wes, good to know in case you do decide to murder me, at least I'll be able to come back and haunt my family, using your name." I wink hoping that the tension I've created will ease.

"One more time, want a ride? We can fetch your vehicle after the storm."

"Thank you, but no."

Wes nods once before heading back to his truck and taking off.

No way was I about to get in a car with a stranger. My parents taught me better than that. Now only if they had taught me what to do in this sort of situation I'd be gold.

Groaning, I threw my head back and closed my eyes. Hopefully Jessy is able to reach someone to come rescue me.

I must have dosed off because I awoke to howling winds. Scared me so bad I thought my heart was going to jump out of my chest.

I can hardly see out of the windshield, rain is

pelting down hard now. I reach over for my phone, it has been over an hour since I talked to my cousin. There are no texts, no missed calls, and no damn bars of service.

Maybe I should have taken Wes's offer. The tow company should have been here by now.

Sighing, I hold my cell up toward the roof and try to dial Jessy for what feels like the hundredth time.

Nothing. Nada.

FOUR

A knock on my window startles me and I scream out like a little bitch.

All I see is bright yellow. Someone in bright yellow. The tow company. Thank goodness.

However, when I open the door, I'm not greeted by a tow company rep, nope. It's Wesley or Wes, whatever.

"Listen, I can't in good faith leave you out here in this weather. Just come back with me and I'll send a tow company first thing when the storm passes."

I eye him up and down. He's no longer rocking the Santa get up. The beard and hat are gone. Wes is wearing a yellow raincoat, unbuttoned. Underneath he's wearing a gray tee that hugs his chest and stomach in all the right places. Plus it helps that I know what he looks like under that shirt. He's still wearing his denim shorts and sneakers.

"Come on Tamera, you don't want to be out here when the snow starts to fall."

"Snow? How cold?"

Wait, he remembered my name. But seriously snow?

"Very cold. First big snow storm of the year is coming, now let's go."

Wes stands there, holding his hand out for me. I should just go. It has to be better than listening to this wind and the possibility of me freezing to death isn't how I pictured dying. I think I'd rather him murder me. At least this way I could die looking at his amazing body.

His large hand engulfs mine as I step out of my SUV, his grip firm. Maybe it's just me but there is something about the way a man holds a woman's hand, as if being protective.

We make a beeline for his truck and while I had hoped to stay semi dry, that didn't happen.

I'm now soaked and cold.

"Shit, I should've given you my raincoat." Wes's voice is laced with regret.

"No, it's fine, I can just grab my change of clothes out of my—"

Bag. The bag that is back in my car. The one I just ran from.

Great thinking Tamera.

"Let me guess, it is in your car?"

"Yup."

"I'll go get it."

"You don't have—"

Before I can finish, he's already out and running back to get my bag. Such a gentlemen and less murder like. Maybe this won't be so bad.

When he climbs back in, he pulls the bag out from under his coat. He kept it dry. I'm impressed. Tanner would have never.

"Thank you."

"No problem."

He starts the truck and turns on the heat. I'm grateful because I'm low key shivering and trying my hardest to hide it.

The ten minute drive to his house is quiet, however when we pull up his driveway, I don't see a house. I see nothing but a red dirt path that is lined with trees and it's very dark. It totally has me rethinking the murderer theory.

❄

We continue on the dark path until we come to a clearing. Smack in the center is a cabin. A huge cabin.

"This is your place?'

"Yup."

"Why so far away from the main road?" I know I shouldn't ask, it's just curiosity gets the best of me.

"I like secluded. I don't want to hear traffic and neighbors. I want peace and quiet."

"Hmm." Sounds a little boring for this Florida girl, but I don't press further.

"Stay there, I'll go grab an umbrella."

"No, it's okay, I'm already soaked."

He nods once as he grabs my bag to put

under his raincoat, then hops out of the truck and comes around to my side and opens the door.

We once again make a dash for it. I nearly slip when I run up the steps, but Wes catches me, bringing our body's mighty close and dang if he isn't as solid as he looks. His masculine, woodsy scent invades my nostrils. I could drink him in with how good he smells.

His hard body engulfs mine, strong arms wrap around me tightly. It's an unfamiliar feeling, yet it feels oddly comforting and electrifying all at once.

"Ya gotta be careful, rain and steps can be dangerous."

"Noted."

He continues holding me, his blue eyes piercing into mine. Neither of us looks away. I realize my heartbeat is racing but it has to be from nearly slipping and falling right?

Clearing my throat, he quickly stands me up and makes sure I'm good before finally letting go.

Upon opening the front door, I step into a massive high ceiling living room. It's minimally decorated. Typical for a guy.

"I'll show you to your room."

Room? I get a room? Shoot, I was totally okay with settling on the couch.

Wes stops at a door on the right of a rather long hallway.

I'm not expecting the size of the bedroom when we walk in. It's huge. I mean I guess I should have because the whole cabin is large, but this room is double the size of the room in my condo back home and that's a master.

"Bathroom is just through that door." Wes points to a door on the other end of the room, near the window.

Wait, there's a bathroom attached?! I quickly go over to it, sure enough. It's not too large, even so, there is plenty of space.

"I hope this is okay."

I turn back to look at him. Is he nervous?

"This is more than okay. I assumed I was sleeping on a couch." Or beneath the ground. I don't mention that part though.

He laughs and shakes his head, "No, I have a guest room so that when my little sister comes to visit, she has her own room."

"That's very kind of you, Wesley.

"Call me Wes. Towels are under the cabinet, I'll leave you to it."

"Thanks."

A shower sounds perfect, especially since I'm still wet and cold.

SIX

The shower felt amazing. Like truly amazing. The hot water took the chill right out of my body.

Now here I stand, in a fresh pair of sweats, some cute Christmas socks, and an oversized red sweater.

What do I do now? Do I go out there or do I just stay in here? I tried Jessy again, but with one bar, it only rang once and then disconnected me so I sent a text once again. Maybe it will eventually go through.

I walk to the door to peek out but stop short when I hear a voice. A woman's voice. Shoot. Maybe Wes has a girlfriend or worse, a wife. I'm sure someone has snatched that piece of eye candy right up.

I debate for a second, not really knowing what to do. I curse my SUV for leaving me stranded and putting me in this position. I should blame Tanner. He had to be a damn deadbeat boyfriend with no direction. I also blame myself, how was I too blind to see our relationship not going anywhere after a year.

A knock on the door startles me.

When I open it, I'm expecting Wes, not some tiny girl with purple hair with a huge smile plastered across her lips that are covered in bright pink lipstick.

"Hi! I'm Ames! It's so nice to meet you!"

"Um... nice to meet you too.." I'm confused.

"Wesley mentioned you were beautiful, but damn."

"Thank you?" I don't know what to even say. Who is this chick and where did Wes go?

I watch as she walks past me into the room and hops right up on the bed. Seriously, is this how people do things up here?

"So Wesley said your car broke down. He'll get it fixed up like new in no time. He's a genius like that."

"How so?"

"He's a mechanic silly." She laughs loudly, a little too loudly.

"Oh, he never mentioned it." Wes didn't tell

me he was a mechanic, he just said he would send for a tow truck.

"Figures. He has never been one to gloat about his successful business. That's not who he is."

I nod. He most definitely doesn't act like some big shot business man.

Just then, Wes comes up to the door. He's freshly showered with a towel draped over his shoulder, no shirt, and a pair of grey sweats.

Hot damn. My eyes roam up and down his body, taking in the hardness of it.

"Ames, come on, I told you not to bother her. Tamera, I'm sorry if she's been harassing you." Wesley runs a hand through his dark wet hair. I know he's not trying to be seductive on purpose, but damn he can make a girl's panties wet just by standing there like that.

"Wesley, it's fine. Isn't it fine, Tamera?" Ames huge eyes beam at me.

"Umm, yeah, totally fine." I lie. I don't want to hurt the chick's feelings, especially if this is his girlfriend. I don't need to give her a reason to throw me out.

It's one night. I can do one night.

"So will you be staying in Wesley's room?"

"I'm sorry?" I nearly choke the words out.

"This is my room. I mean you can totally crash with me, but I think you'll enjoy sleeping with Wes, better." Ames winks at me as she hops back down off the bed. She goes and grabs a bag that was sitting by the doorway. I had totally missed it until now.

I turn back to see Wesley, shock evident on his face as his crystal blue eyes meet mine.

"Come on, I'll show you to my room." He huffs as he turns to walk away.

Umm.. his room..

"Wait.. She said I can crash with her?"

Wes comes in close, so close I can see the beads of water that hang at the tips of his messy brown hair.

"Trust me, you do not want to share a room with my sister."

"Wha— why not? She seems fine."

"She finds clothes, what's the word, restricting. She's a nudist, so to speak, and sleeps naked. She will most likely be stripping out of clothes any minute now.

Wesley smirks once before turning to head back down the hall, leaving me standing there with my mouth gaped open.

SEVEN

I follow Wesley to his room that is clear across the cabin. I pause once I get to his doorway. I can totally just crash on the couch. I turn to look at the furniture in the living room, there is no real couch, just a love seat and a few chairs. Well, shit.

"Are you coming?" His husky voice questions from somewhere in the room.

Forcing my feet to move, I walk in and notice two things.

One- his bed is massive. The bed frame is made out of logs, just like the house, and it's covered by a black and red checkered comforter.

Two- him.

Yes, him. Wes. He's standing in the doorway

to what I assume leads to the bathroom. There's a light on that casts a glow over him. At the moment, he looks delectable, like a chocolate dessert that I would happily eat and then lick the plate clean.

"See something you want?"

Ommgeee, Wes caught me checking him out.

"What? No." My face heats, betraying me.

"No sense in denying it, Tamera. I caught you staring."

Hot damn, he's blunt.

"I.. wasn't, I didn't mean too—" I stop short as he starts walking toward me.

"We will be sharing a bed together, so unless you want me bending you over the bed, you will need to get your thoughts in check."

Holy shit.

That was hot.

But he's a stranger. I don't have sex with strangers, do I? I mean I could, I am single after all and what's one night of a little fun? It's been so long since I have just let loose. I've been too busy stressing over my shit relationship. What's one night? I'm stuck here, might as well make the most of it.

Arousal runs through my body as I picture Wes naked, bending me over the bed. Swallowing my nerves, I step closer, "Maybe that's what I want."

"Tamera," He warns, the humor in his eyes turns hungry as they roam over my chest.

"Wes."

I go to reach out and touch the hard ridges of his chest, but he grabs my wrist stopping me.

"You're playing with fire,"

"Maybe I want to." I wink taking a step closer so that I am completely in his personal space. Wes smells clean, his woodsy scent has been washed away in the shower. He's so much taller than me too.

"Tamera, I gotta warn you, I only fuck."

"Even better."

Who is this girl inside of me and where has she been hiding?

He growls as he takes a step back, clearly needing space from me. I glance down and notice the growing bulge inside his sweats. It's large. Much larger than Tanner's.

Wes grabs himself, causing me to look back up to him. I see the heat in those sky blue eyes of his. He wants me, even though he's trying to resist.

"One night Wes, that's it. No strings attached. I just got out of a relationship and I'm definitely not looking for another one."

I watch as his jaw tightens and how his throat bobs when he swallows. He's taking his time, thinking of what to say to me, all the while the hunger on his face grows.

Wes suddenly storms off past me and out of the room. Maybe this wasn't a good idea?

Of course not Tamera, he is a stranger and could still murder you.

I don't know what else to do, so I go over to the bed and sit down. This isn't weird. Not at all.

He comes back a minute later, my bag is in his hand. He shuts the door behind him, locking it. I heard the click. He most certainly just locked the bedroom door.

Nervous excitement fills me as his eyes lock on mine.

EIGHT

Wes drops my bag by the dresser and comes toward me. It suddenly feels stuffy in here, like I can't breathe.

Wes climbs on the bed and invades my space. His closeness causes me to fall back against the pillows. He doesn't stop until he is hovering above me.

With Wes over me, it's like watching a scene in a steamy movie. Above me, he hovers shirtless, with perfect abs on display. Trailing my eyes lower, his joggers hang low on his hips. His erection strains against the cotton material. It's mouthwatering, let me tell you.

"Is this what you want, Tamera?" His husky voice causes my eyes to pop back up to his.

This is what I want right? A night of random sex to forget all the crap things that have happened lately.

Hell, why not? What's one night?

"Yes.."

I reach a hand up and trace the ridges of his chest. Tanner definitely wasn't built like this. Not even close. Wes reaches out and slowly runs a hand up my sweater, he pauses just beneath my breasts.

"Take this off."

He nods to my sweater.

Grabbing the hem of it, I pull it over my head, exposing my breasts to him. I'm not overly busty, just a C cup. Tanner never complained. Then again, he hardly paid any attention to them. I can't help but wonder what Wes thinks of them?

Looking up at him, I watch as his nostrils flare. There's fire in his eyes. I'd say he approves.

I go back to tracing the ridges of his perfect body.. I could lick whip cream off of him, no questions asked.

When Wes's hand glides up and takes a nipple between his fingers, all thoughts of whip cream go out the window. I throw my head back on the pillows and let out a quiet moan.

I feel his breath hit my chest before his mouth captures a nipple. It sends electricity straight down to my core. He nips and sucks repeatedly for a few seconds before turning his attention to my other nipple. I can't help but claw my hands through his hair.

It's been far too long since my body has been touched like this.

Wes leans back on his legs and in one swift move, yanks my sweats down my legs, tossing them behind him.

Laying here completely naked, Wes eyes my body.

"Fuck," he hisses and somehow that turns me on more.

"Touch me, Wes."

His eyes move to my mouth. I purposely lick my lips, teasing him.

"Tamera..."

"If you won't touch me, I'll touch myself." I trail my hand down, just to gage a reaction from him. Hooded eyes follow my hand. The minute I reach between my folds, he yanks my hand away.

"The fuck you will."

He dips a finger between my already slick folds and pumps it in and out a few times, soaking me more.

He slides his finger out and grips my hips hard, pulling me down further on the bed.

He ducks down, nipping my legs then thighs,

until he comes up to my apex and licks my slit ever so slowly.

"Wes," I moan.

He continues licking and sucking while my hands fist his hair. I'm on the brink of coming undone when his finger plunges into me, sending me straight over the edge.

I scream out his name over and over as my body trembles from my orgasm. He doesn't let up, instead he laps up every ounce of me like a man starved.

Once my trembling slows, he leans up and into the night stand, grabbing a condom.

He slides it on in one swift move and lines himself up.

"Fucking, that's all this is. Don't be getting attached to me." His words may seem serious, but the playful look on his face gives him away.

"Shut up already."

I reach between us, grabbing him myself and arching so just the tip rubs at my entrance. He's so thick in my hand. I'm almost worried that this may hurt a bit.

"Damnit Tamera." He growls and slams into me, hard.

His cock fills me so completely that he stills for a minute as he stretches me. He pulls out slowly before slamming back into me over and over. A mixture between pleasure and pain washes over me. I can't help but grip his strong arms as he continues thrusting in and out.

Wes pulls out fast and flips me over, bringing my hips up. He sticks a finger between my folds once, lubricating me all over again before he thrusts his cock back into me, balls deep.

I moan out as he rocks in and out, over and over, until waves of pleasure wash over me for the second time tonight.

Wes follows quickly behind, his cock jutting as he comes.

I collapse, keeping my eyes shut. Did I really just have sex with a stranger?

Yes, yes I did.

I just had the most mind blowing sex ever.

NINE

When Wes gets off the bed without a word, I half expect him to leave the room and not come back.

Except he doesn't leave the room. I can hear him shuffling around. What do I do now?

Regret starts to creep into my mind, but I shut it down when I hear the faucet. Wes comes back a minute later and begins to clean me up. He's gentle, taking care not to hurt my overly sensitive skin. I'll admit, I would have never expected him to clean me up. Shit, Tanner never did and we were together for how long?

Too long, Tamera.

I chew on my lip, thinking about this situation. I just had sex with a total stranger and then he cleans me up after.

Who does that?

A real man, that's who.

After some time, Wes comes in and settles into the bed. He lies on the complete opposite side from me. I shouldn't expect him to lay next to me or to cuddle with me. Yet, something deep inside of me wishes he was holding me close.

It was just sex.

Just sex. Do not get attached.

I sigh, closing my eyes wanting to reimagine just the way Wes's hands felt on my body. How his tongue felt, all of it—

"Stop thinking and go to sleep."

How does he know that?

"I'm not thinking."

"Yeah, sure. I keep hearing you sigh. Now go to sleep."

Shit. He's paying attention to me.

People who fuck don't pay attention to the other person, do they? Surely not.

A million thoughts swirl in my mind. Wes, my car, and what awaits when I return back to Florida. At the front of my mind though is Wes. I can't stop thinking about how he touched me, how he took my body and devoured me. It's the last thing I picture before drifting off to sleep.

❄

The coldness in the room wakes me. Opening my eyes a little, blinking away the sleep, Panic hits. I sit up fast before remembering I am in Wes's bed. I look over to his spot, it's empty. I'm still naked from last night's events. That must be why I am so cold. I wrap the blanket around me to go in search of my discarded clothes.

I dress in a rush and go in search of coffee and hopefully an update on my SUV.

When I walk into the kitchen, Ames is sitting at the counter with a glass of orange juice in one hand and her cell phone in the other. Her purple hair is up in a bun, no bright lipstick this morning. She's in an oversized sweater and a pair of socks. That's it. Wes's words come back to me. She doesn't like clothes.

"Morning," I quietly mumble.

I don't want to be too loud in case Wes is sleeping elsewhere.

"Well good morning to you too!"

Damn, so much for being quiet.

"Did you sleep well?"

I bite my bottom lip and think about her question. I slept perfectly well with a dull ache between my thighs that I had to squeeze more than once to suppress the need to crawl over to the stranger who laid beside me.

"I know that look!"

Ames jumps up from the stool and slams her

hand on the counter. She looks at me with a huge smile on her face.

"Wha.. what look?"

"You had sex last night!"

Warmth spreads across my face in embarrassment. How can she know we had sex? She doesn't even know me or my facial expressions. Oh my god did she hear us?

No. There's no way. I wasn't loud. At least I don't think I was.

"You did!"

She jumps up and down clapping her hands in excitement. Why on earth is she excited over me having sex with her brother? Shouldn't she be pissed or call me terrible names?

"Um, it's not what you—"

"Oh it sure is! Sex is written all over your face girl!"

I groan and put my head in my hands. Is it really that noticeable? Ames makes it sounds like I have a giant sign stuck to my forehead that reads "I had sex".

"Was it good? Wait! Don't tell me, it's my brother, that would be weird."

"Oh my god." I groan out with my head still hiding in my hands. I can't face her. Hell, I don't even know if I want to face Wes now. I just need to get my vehicle so I can get out of here and get to my cousin's place.

"Do you have any idea what this means, Tamera?"

"Um, it means nothing."

"Wes has a thing for you."

I slowly peel my hands away from my face. I thought Ames was off her rocker before, but her statement confirms that she is officially crazy.

"Uh yeah, sure. Look, it's not like that. It was just one time. We don't even know each other."

"I'm telling you right now, he has a thing for you."

I sigh, no point in debating with a certified crazy chick.

"Have you seen him?"

"He went to tow your car before the next storm rolls through."

"Next storm?"

Ames flicks her hand in the air, "Yeah, last night's storm was just a teaser for what's coming. No predicting this weather sometimes."

"Does that mean my car won't be ready?"

"Probably not. Wes has just enough time to drop it off at the shop and get back here before the blizzard comes through."

I pull up my phone, needing to check the weather. Somehow by the grace of 5G, I am able to see what's coming. Shit. I study the screen for a minute trying to understand the impending weather.

This Florida girl is stuck. One might say screwed, no pun intended.

Great.

This is great.

Looks like I'll be staying another night with Wes.

TEN

I need to call Jessy. She is probably wondering what has happened to me. For all I know, she has sent a search party out to find me. How humiliating would that be?

After two rings she answers, sounding panicked.

"Tamera! Are you okay? Please tell me you are okay!"

"I am. It's a long story, but a passerby picked me up and I crashed at his cabin."

"HIS! You are with a man? Oh my god! I should have checked the forecast before having you come. Are you safe? Do you feel safe?"

"Yes, yes, I'm fine. This guy, Wes, has been

very kind and his sister is here too. He actually owns a mechanic shop according to his sister—"

Shrieks through the line cut off my words. What in the hell is she freaking out over?

"Jessy, what on Earth?"

"Are you with Wesley Thompson? Do you have any idea who he is?!"

I swallow the panic that is rising in my throat.

"Please tell me I'm not staying with a murderer?" I whisper so no one walking by the room will hear.

"What?! God No! The complete opposite. You are staying with Helen's most eligible bachelor."

"Come again?"

"Everyone wants Wesley, but no one has caught his eye. He doesn't date either. All he does is work."

"Hmm..." I say more to myself than to my cousin.

Wes is single, that much I knew, well figured anyway. I'm not quite sure how to process this other bit of information.

"He's hot isn't he? All muscle wrapped up in a delicious package."

Ha, leave it to Jessy, she's always so blunt.

"He sure is hot."

I tell her as I stare out the window, watching the snow flurries fall lightly. It's not snowing hard yet but watching the wind carry the flurries in different directions, I assume it won't be long before the storm arrives.

"Anyways, I was calling you because I guess another storm is going to be coming and my SUV won't be ready."

"Listen, being stranded with that man might not be such a bad thing. He's a nice piece of eye candy."

Don't I know it? She would go nuts if I told her I slept with him. I smile at the thought of telling her. However, that's a story for another day.

Realization starts to sink in that I will be staying with him again and most likely in his bed. I wonder if it'll be another night of mind blowing sex. I sure hope so.

"Girl you got it bad, I can hear it in the way you sigh."

"What, no I don't, I just said he was hot. That's all."

"So I'm hot?"

I go stiff as a deep masculine voice sounds from behind me. How long has he been standing there? Or worse, how much did he hear? Could he hear Jessy's loud mouth?

"Hey, listen Jessy I gotta let you go. I'll call you back."

"Uh huh. I bet the eye candy is around."

She is relentless so I shake my head and end the call. I know he's still behind me, I can feel him. I have no choice but to take a deep breath, smile and turn around to face him.

"Oh hey, didn't know you were back." I say before turning to him and holy shit am I not prepared for what is standing in front of me.

Wes stands in the doorway, arms stretched above his head, holding the top of the door frame. It's a shame he is wearing layers because I bet, no I know his chiseled arms would be on display.

He's got a black beanie on his head that his dark hair peeks out from. Jessy is right, he is a nice piece of eye candy.

"You think I'm hot, but that's all, huh?"

My face heats in embarrassment as I try to think of what to say back.

"So you heard that?"

"I did."

"I, um..." I trail off and cast my eyes down, unsure of what to say. I feel like a kid in the candy store who just got caught taking candy.

"Look at me, Tamera."

I do as he says, I'm not sure why but I do and when I look up I see the heat flicker in his eyes. He stands there saying nothing, just staring. It's kind of intimidating to have someone so beautiful stare at someone like me. Little ol' me.

"Your vehicle will not be ready today, the

storm that was supposed to come through last night ended up being a preview for what's coming later today. You'll be staying with me again." Wes pauses with a smirk across his face.

I swallow, he confirms what Ames and the weather app already told me. My brain says I should try and fight this. I mean, can't he drive me to Jessy's? It shouldn't be super far from here. Of course I have no idea where I'm at though and she could be clear across town.

Instead, I only nod in return. This means another night with those piercing eyes staring deep into my soul like they are right now.

"In my bed." His arms drop from the door as he turns and walks out before I can respond.

Holy shit.

ELEVEN

Wes leaves me standing there in his room in complete shock. Many questions and scenarios run through my mind, especially after repeating his last words over and over.

In my bed.

I'll be in his bed with him again. Just that thought alone has me squeezing my thighs together. It was supposed to be one night. Just one night of meaningless fun.

Okay so maybe it'll turn into two nights of casual sex or in his eyes fucking. I close my eyes, he definitely fucked me last night. It was rough and raw, yet it was easily the best sex I had ever had.

Ames calls out my name, distracting me from

my thoughts. It's a good thing, I need to focus on something other than Wes.

"Yeah?" I say as I walk out of the room, stopping when I see her.

"Um, why are you in a bikini?"

Seriously? Why? Does she not realize how cold it is outside? There's even a chill inside, hence the reason I am still in my sweater and sweats.

"Because we are gonna get in the jacuzzi, Come on!"

She seems excited over this. A little too excited as she stands there. She's tall and lean. She's wearing a purple and black striped bikini. The purple is almost the exact shade as her hair and I can't help but wonder if she planned it that way.

"Grab your suit, come on. Wesley is already in."

"He's outside in the jacuzzi?"

"Yup, hurry."

"Wait, I don't have a swim suit. I didn't think coming to Georgia for Christmas would entail needing one."

She tips her head back laughing.

"Jacuzzi's in the winter are exactly why you need one."

"Oh."

"Well grab a tank and a pair of panties. No big deal or you could always go commando."

"Um," I shift nervously, thinking about Wes seeing me.

"Relax, you've already had sex Wesley. Which by the way is a really big deal. Now go change."

"Okay, okay." I stand there watching as she turns to leave. She isn't just in a bikini, but a g-string bikini at that. She has no shame.

I quickly comb through my bag to find a navy tank. It's thin but it will have to do. Unfortunately, all I have are thongs, so my ass is going to be on display, just like Ames. I tell myself I can do this as I slip a pink pair on. My nerves have kicked into high gear, especially hearing Ames say that sex with Wes was a big deal. What is that supposed to mean? I have all these questions and no one is giving me answers.

I'm freezing as I walk out of the room, feeling self conscious. I can't believe I'm about to get in a jacuzzi while snow is slowly falling and it's like zero degrees outside. Okay, maybe not zero degrees, but to this Florida girl, it sure feels that way.

"Oh good, you found something and wow. I can't wait to see Wesley's reaction."

"I'm not sure about this. I'm freezing."

Ames loops an arm through mine as she goes

to open his back door that I now see opens to a very large deck. In the corner sits the jacuzzi and sure enough, Wes is in it, his head thrown back, eyes closed. He looks relaxed.

"We'll only be cold for a few seconds. The quicker we get in the warmer we'll be."

"Yeah, sure."

Wes pops his head up upon hearing the door shut. His eyes go wide the minute he spots me. I hurry behind Ames and watch as his eyes drink me in from head to toe. He pauses on my chest, staring at my erect nipples before trailing his eyes down lower. I watch as his jaw tightens.

"What are you doing Ames?" He asks without taking his blue eyes off of my body.

"Joining you, what's it look like?"

I am shivering as I go to take up and into the steamy, hot water but I slip slightly and almost lose my balance. Wes moves fast and catches my arm, gripping it tightly to prevent me from falling completely.

That's not embarrassing, not at all.

He continues to hold my arm guiding me into the water. I feel his eyes on me the entire time. Once I'm in, I sink down to wear my head is the only thing above the water. I welcome the warmth as it takes over my body.

When I glance over to Ames, I see her

smiling with a twinkle in her eye. She's up to something. I just know it. I feel it.

"You know what, I think I'm going to go in and do some decorating. Ya know, get in the Christmas spirit. Maybe I'll bake too."

"Ames, I thought—"

"Let her go." Wes cuts me off while staring at his sister. It's like there's some silent communication going on between them and I'm on the outside. I'm starting to, I don't know, feel like she totally set me up to get me to come out here with Wes.

Are they in on this together?

TWELVE

The minute Ames shuts the door, Wes is on me. His arm snakes around my middle as he pulls me close to him. I follow his eyes as they once again trail down to my chest. The wet fabric of my shirt clings to my breasts, revealing my hard nipples more now than when my tank was dry. I glance back up to him to find him still staring at them, the muscles in his jaw jump with each swallow he takes. I sort of like this effect I'm having on him. Especially since talking to Jessy earlier.

He pulls me even closer, wrapping my legs around his waist. His erection brushes across my thong, sending electricity throughout my body. I grind, wanting to feel more of him.

"Tamera," He warns through clenched teeth as he holds my hips to keep me from moving.

I raise an eyebrow, no way he is gonna stop me, not when he's drooling over my breasts and rock hard.

In one swift move, I'm off his lap and being spun around to where my back is against his chest. One hand still grips my hip the other is now on my thigh while I now feel his hardness rubbing on my ass.

I wait in anticipation as his hand roams up my thigh and then slides under my thong. His finger teases my clit, rubbing circles. Now instead of grinding into his cock, I find myself grinding into his hand as my head falls back on his shoulder as pleasure takes over. Wes nips and sucks on my neck as his movements quicken. He's sucking so hard that he has to be leaving marks, yet I don't even care.

"Wes," I moan out as I start to tremble.

He must know I'm close because he dips a finger into me while keeping his thumb on my swollen clit.

Wes says nothing though, just keeps up his assault on my neck and collarbone while his hand brings me over the edge. I can't stop the loud moans that escape as I fall apart to his touch. Squeezing my eyes shut, all I see is white, but what I feel in that moment is anything but.

My body is on fire, I want Wes inside of me, now. I try to turn around to face him, but he holds me in place.

"Wes, I want you inside of me." I whimper.

"Later."

His words are like a punch in the gut.

"Why later?" I ask while attempting to get out of his grip.

He holds me in place and leans into my ear.

"Because Tamera, When my cock is buried inside of you, I want to see it. I want to watch your pussy take all of me and right now that's impossible, so you'll just have to be patient and wait until later."

Well then.

THIRTEEN

The rest of the afternoon goes by in a blur. I had lunch with Ames. We made small talk. But truthfully, I don't remember what we even talked about. I couldn't even tell you if she did any Christmas decorating at all.

All I keep thinking about are the words that Wes whispered to me before he gave me another orgasm. This is totally normal for two strangers who just fuck, completely normal. Though, there's this little voice from somewhere in my head that keeps saying it could be more. I shut that down real quick. Nope. It can't be more and it won't be. I seriously need to think about other things. Something that does not involve Wes or his cock.

Laying in Wes's bed, I watch the snow, now falling harder, whipping in the wind as darkness begins to take over. The view is absolutely beautiful. I've never seen so much snow and know I probably wouldn't survive here. I belong on the beach basking in the sun. And just like when the snow storm is over and forgotten, Wes will become a distant faded memory.

"What are you thinking about?"

I sit up, I didn't even hear him come in.

"I was just thinking about the snow, why?"

"You looked sad."

"Oh..."

His words stir something inside of me, I'm not sure why. I also don't know how I feel about him being able to read my face. He doesn't even know me.

I watch him as he kneels down in front of the fireplace that I didn't even notice until now and start placing fire wood in it.

"It's going to get really cold tonight."

"I guess it's a good thing you got me to keep you warm." I tease.

"Is that so?"

"Yup."

He laughs and shakes his head as he continues working on getting the fire going. His laughter makes me smile. I'm beginning to like my stay here at Wesley Thompson's cabin and a strange feeling creeps in when I think about leaving when the storm is over.

"Why the scowl?"

"Nothing,"

"Didn't look like nothin'." Wes raises an eyebrow and studies me before coming over next to me on the bed. I have to scoot over to allow him to sit down comfortably. His masculine scent rolls off of him and let me tell you, it's enough to make my mouth water.

"Tell me something about you, your age, birthdate, anything?"

"I'm twenty-six, you?'

Wes hesitates for a moment, "I'm thirty-two."

I nod, I've never been with a guy more than a few years older than me and I'll admit, I think I've been missing out.

"Are you enjoying yourself so far?" He is quick to change the subject.

Biting my bottom lip, I nod once. There's no way I can speak words. They would betray me because in my mind I'd like to tell him that I'm enjoying his cock very much and his mouth too. Since I can't say things out loud, it's best I just nod.

Wes's eyes never leave my face. I know what he is doing. He's trying to read me, figure me out. I'm just not sure why.

I watch as Wes stands from the bed and

disappears into the bathroom. I'm kind of thankful for the silence because he has my mind all sorts of fucked up. We are just having some fun until this storm blows over. He doesn't even know my last name, nor does he know that I do not even live in this state.

Wes comes back a few minutes later, dressed in yet another pair of gray sweats. I can just barely see the outline of his cock.

"I see you."

Damnit. That man is always catching me as I check him out.

I smile, "I like what I see."

He comes over top of me, his arms on each side of me, holding his body weight. I wish he wasn't wearing the white thermal tee that he has on. I want to see his chest. His muscular chest.

"Oh yeah?"

"Yup."

He leans back on his knees and grabs my hips, pulling me further down the bed. When his hand leaves my hip and moves up my shirt, he leans down, to bite my neck.My heart rate speeds up. I know I want more of this, of that I'm sure. Especially after what played out in the jacuzzi.

I grab the hem of my sweater and pull it over my head to give him better access of my breasts, of me.

"Just fucking," He whispers more to himself than to me and that surprises me.

I shake the thoughts that start to run through my mind as soon as his hand begins to touch me in places that make everything else fall away. And that's just what we do. With the snow falling outside and the fire going inside, we get lost in each other over and over.

FOURTEEN

We lay here holding each other for a few minutes, both of us drenched in sweat. We say nothing. No words are needed. I'm afraid words will make me feel things I shouldn't. Is that crazy? Crazy that he makes me want to feel something more than just casual sex?

Unfortunately, Wes breaks the silence all too soon.

"Would you like me to run you a shower? I can get one going for you."

Who is this Wesley Thompson and where has he been for all of my adult life?

When I tell him I'd like to take another shower, he nods and goes back to the bathroom. He's still naked so I take this time to sit up and watch his toned ass, thick legs move with each step he takes. The sight alone has me growing wet all over again.

Shit girl. Get it together.

"Tamera," Wes calls from the bathroom.

Getting up, I follow his steps until I reach his gigantic bathroom. My breath catches the minute I spot Wes. There he stands still naked, holding the shower door open for me.

"Are you going to get in or are you just going to stare at me?"

"Are you coming in with me?"

"Yes, if that's okay with you." A smile plays on his lips. Lips I've never tasted. I suddenly want to taste them.

This seems intimate. I know we just had sex, but this is too intimate. This is something lovers do.

"Um.. Do you think this is a good idea? Us together in a shower?"

Wes lets out a laugh and not just a little chuckle. He throws his head back, full on laughing.

"What's so funny?"

"We just fucked Tamera and you are worried about getting in the shower with me? That's a little silly? Don't you think?"

He's right. Damnit. I shrug still not moving.

"Get in the shower, now."

For some reason, his demand sends electricity straight down to my core which in turn, causes my feet to move toward the huge shower. Plus I'm freezing, standing here naked.

Wes reaches a hand around my waist to guide me in. I don't know why, but I allow him to and ask no more questions.

The water is warm and soothing. Closing my eyes, I smell the faint scent of vanilla.

Without a word, Wes starts washing me with a cloth. He starts with my shoulders and back, then moves to my front. He does nothing except clean me in the sweetest, most intimate way. I lean back allowing him to finish bathing me.

Never and I repeat never has any man done this to me. It's like I've been with all the wrong men and finally met a man who knows how to treat and care for a woman.

I shouldn't get too excited over it though. Wes and I are strangers who live in two different worlds. This will never amount to anything. This is nothing more than sex. So why is my heart beating so hard that it feels like it is going to burst through my chest at any moment?

FIFTEEN

"Wake up sleepy head." A female's voice whispers in my ear. It's a dream I tell myself as I roll over away from the voice.

"Tamera, come on. We are going into town soon. You need to be dressed and ready, otherwise Wesley will get grumpy."

I sit up fast, my breathing hard. It wasn't a dream. There is a woman standing over me.

Ames.

She laughs a little.

"You are so cute. Now come on. Start getting dressed."

"Wait where are we going?" I ask as I rub my eyes trying to focus more.

"We are going to see the Festival of the Trees

today and bring home a Christmas tree to decorate."

Her face is full of excitement, like a child who is about to open presents. I get a little excited until I realize this isn't real life. What about my SUV and Jessy?

She starts to pull the blankets back, but I grab them. I'm still naked from the waist down. After the shower, Wes put me in one of his thermal tops and then brought me to ecstasy with his tongue once more before sleep finally consumed us both.

Ames must sense my panic because she giggles and shakes her head. Shouldn't she be pissed that I'm screwing her brother?

"Girl you both got it bad."

I shake my head. I can't. I can't have these thoughts or this conversation with her. Focus Tamera.

"What about my SUV? I should probably get going to my cousin's."

"Yeah, okay. Wes has people working on it today. That much I know." She shrugs like it is no big deal and heads for the door.

"Do you have warm clothes to venture out in?"

"Um..." I mean I have jeans and sweaters and a pair of sneakers. I wasn't planning on going anywhere.

"That's what I thought, let me go roam my closet."

I lay back on the bed and sigh. What kind of Christmas breakdown is this turning into?

Less than ten minutes later, Ames reappears with an outfit. She hands me a solid green sweater, and a black coat that she paired with black skinny jeans and a pair of black duck boots. I couldn't have picked anything out of my bag that even comes close to being this trendy.

"Oh and here's a scarf and gloves." She tosses them on the bed and practically dances her way out of the room.

She reminds me of Jessy. How the two of them have so much energy is beyond me. However, I do know that I need to get my ass in gear before grumpy Wes comes in. I giggle, part of me kind of wants to see who grumpy Wes is.

I'm putting the finishing touches on my eyeliner when I feel his presence. I turn to find him at the edge of the room, head tilted, watching me. His expression is unreadable even though I see I twinkle in those sky blue eyes of his. He is dressed in a pair of black jeans himself with a red flannel button down. He's holding a Santa hat in his hands. I almost want to ask what it is for, then remembering how we first met, I don't need to ask. Wes is strange like that and hot. So fucking hot. He looks like something straight out of a magazine.

"Are you ready"

I turn back to the mirror, "Just about. I hear we are going to some Christmas tree thing."

"We are."

That's it. He gives nothing else away.

"Any update on my vehicle?"

He says nothing and for a second I think maybe he walked out of the room, but when I turn to check. He's still standing there, unmoving, just watching me. His stare gives me chills. I'm just not sure if I should be excited or fearful.

"Wes,"

"The guys are working on it now to see what the actual problem is. Once we narrow it down, I will give you an update on when it will be done."

I sigh, closing my eyes. This isn't how my trip was supposed to go. Not that I'm totally complaining, I mean I've had some amazing sex, it's just, I feel like I'm intruding.

"I can take you to your cousin's after the festival."

My eyes snap open, "You would do that?"

"I would. Are you not happy staying here?"

"It's not that, it's just, this breakdown wasn't part of my plan. I mean I'm grateful you took me in. Really. I just don't want to impose on you."

I stop trying to explain myself before I look

like a fool with my rambling. Wes comes up close to me, so close that his scent comes off him, intoxicating my mind.

"Has Ames made you feel unwelcome here?"

"No, of course not."

"Have I once made you feel like I didn't want you here?"

"No.. not at all." I shake my head.

His face is so close to mine. It's never been this close. We've never kissed. He's never kissed me above my neck, but right now, in this moment, his lips are so close to mine as his breath dances across my nose and lips. If I were to lean in just a tiny bit, our lips would touch.

"That's what I thought." Wes sounds restrained as the words leave his lips.

"Wes..." I trail off unsure of what to say. I really should just kiss him, but what if he doesn't kiss me back? He obviously isn't a kisser.

"Tamera,"

Wes speaks my name so seductively, his hand comes up around the back of my neck, gripping it gently. His lips barely brush mine, just barely, but I feel them.

"Okay you two love birds, I hate to break ya'll up but we need to be going."

Wes pulls away immediately as Ames's voice breaks the bubble we were just in, leaving my body feeling like it is on fire. Instantly, I reach out touching my lips. We were so close. If Ames hadn't come in I am certain we would have kissed right then and there.

Without another word, Wes grabs my hand and leads me out of the room and out of the house to start our adventure.

An adventure I'm not sure I want to end just yet.

SIXTEEN

The Christmas tree festival was amazing. A layer of white covered the grounds and rooftops. It was magical and unlike anything I've ever seen in Florida. I took it all in while Wes walked next to me wearing his Santa hat proudly.

A lot of people came up to him, and each time he introduced me as Tamera. No one pressed further on who I was, not even the women who flocked up to him batting their fake lashes. While I was grateful no one asked about me further, I was a little uncomfortable, okay maybe a little jealous of the amount of women who came up to him, trying to steal his attention. He paid them no mind really, keeping his hand on my lower back. And let me tell ya, those women noticed where his hand was. Every last one of them stopped and stared for a moment glaring. I felt relief each time they sauntered off. I don't know why I even feel this way, it's not like Wes and I are anything, yet for some reason I do.

Ames picked out a tree, a huge tree. Wes just laughed and agreed to it. I was almost certain it wasn't going to fit in his cabin, but looking at it now as the two of them decorate it, It's the perfect size.

"Come help Tamera!" Ames pulls me up off the couch. She takes my hot cocoa out of my hands and replaces it with an ornament.

"Oh, I don't know about this, I mean I'm sort of out of place here." I try to whisper to her, but I know Wes heard it because his expression just went from playful to hard real quick.

Shit.

"Nonsense, my brother likes you." She winks at me as she says the words.

Wes likes me? That can't be right, he doesn't know me and according to Jessy, he's Helen, Georgia's most eligible guy. Yeah, there's no way he likes some damsel in distress.

"Ames," Wes warns.

"What? I'm just helping you two stubborn mules out. You like her, you just don't want to admit it, you're afraid."

He glares at her for all of five seconds before

shaking his head and turning his attention back to the evergreen.

"So Tamera, how long are you staying around for?"

Ames is fishing for information, I can tell. The question is, did Wes put her up to this? I doubt it. He has been pretty blunt with me. If he wanted to know, he would ask me himself.

"Um, well my plans were to stay until after Christmas and then return home."

"Ooh fun! Where is home? Like South Georgia?"

"More like central Florida." I say as I hand Ames an ornament to hang.

"You live in Florida?" Wes's words hang in the air, thick and suffocating. I look to Ames like she can offer me some sort of advice.

"Yeah, I was driving up to stay with my cousin for the holiday when I broke down and you found me."

His jaw tightens for a moment before he storms out of the room.

"Ames, what was that about?" I lean in and whisper to her because I really don't want him to hear me this time.

"I don't know, but I think you need to go find out."

My feet are planted in place. I can't move, not even when she gives me a little push.

"Go on Tamera, obviously, Wesley wants to discuss this and he wants to do so in private."

I sigh, she's right. I should at least go talk to the man who seems upset by my revelation. I'm not sure why he is upset though. His exact words come back to me, "We're just fucking."

I knock on his bedroom door once, before peaking my head in. He's in front of the massive window, staring out. The snow has started falling again.

"Wes, are you okay?"

I quietly close the door behind me before walking to stand next to him. For a while, no words are spoken. We both just stand there, staring out, lost in our own thoughts.

He's the first to break the silence, "I figured you lived in Georgia, just not in Helen."

"I live just south of Cocoa Beach, Florida. I came up here so I didn't have to spend the holiday alone."

"Do you not have family in Florida?"

"I do, my parents live in North Florida, they are in Canada though."

"Why didn't you go with them?"

"I just got out of a relationship and they already had Canada planned. I couldn't pull it off."

Wes nods once before finally turning to look at me.

"Let's go to bed."

Okay, this took a strange turn, but I decide to just roll with it.

I refuse to let my heart think that Wes was upset at the fact that I do not live nearby.

Don't get attached, Remember that.

SEVENTEEN

I change quickly and climb into bed, laying next to a shirtless Wes. How he can go with no shirt is beyond me. This Florida girl doesn't do cold.

Wes pulls me close to his chest, not letting go of me. As much as I shouldn't enjoy this closeness, I do.

"I kind of like having you in my bed."

His words shock me. Did he say what I think he did? His husky voice replays in my head. He did. He definitely said he kind of likes having me in his bed.

"Really now?"

"Yes, and I don't let anyone in my bed. Ever."

I sit up and face him, now it's my turn to study him. He's got a smirk on his face which makes it hard for me to process his words. He sounded very serious when he spoke a moment ago.

"You're joking?"

"Not at all." Adventure dances in those sky blue eyes of his along with something else that I can't quite put my finger on.

"I thought we were just fucking." I use air quotes to make a point of his exact words.

"That was before I had a taste of you, Tamera."

Oh.

Oh fucking my.

"Why did you storm off when I mentioned that I lived in Florida?"

"Reality hit with your words that what's happening between us will go nowhere."

For some reason his words sting, but the look on his face, it hurts. Sadness seeps out of him like a sickness. It's hard to look at him, the sparkle in his eyes has dimmed.

"Did you.. did you expect this to go somewhere, Wes?"

"Not at first, no."

"So you want this to go somewhere now?"

"Not at first, no."

Same response, though his tone is strained, serious.

"Oh."

"I haven't had a relationship in a very long time. My last girlfriend up and moved across the country without so much as a word. It crushed me, I was planning on making her my wife, I wanted her to have my babies."

He stares at the ceiling as he speaks, clearly this is hard for him to talk about. I stay quiet to allow him to continue, not wanting to interrupt.

"After her, I swore off relationships. I didn't want anything to do with connecting with anyone. You came along, I thought I was just helping you out for a day, but then Ames showed up putting us in close proximity. I tried to tell myself not to feel anything, but it's hard." Wes pauses before looking back to me. "I don't even know you, but you make me feel things, Tamera. You make me feel a lot of things and knowing I'm just a pit stop before you go back to Florida sucks."

Holy shit. This man just exposed his feelings to me. Without thinking, I climb on top of him and let my hands roam his body.

"I don't know you either, Wes. What I do know is that I've never been with a man the way I have been with you. I've never had a man claim my body the way you have. The way you touch me, how you are rough one minute and then gentle the next. I've never experienced that. I have never once had anyone devour my body the way you have. You rough hands touch me and I come alive."

I slide down his body, taking his sweats with me. As I spoke my honesty, I could feel him harden beneath me. My body aches, wanting him. But first, I need to do something.

I take his length in my hand, stroking it slowly. Wes sucks in a breath as I lick the tip, licking the little bit of pre-cum that's pooled there.

"Tamera," He growls out, grabbing a fist of my hair.

"Mmm" I respond back as my mouth envelopes his throbbing cock. He's huge and while I know there is no way I can take all of him, I damn near try. I continue the slow motion, sliding up and down his cock until he pulls at my hair.

"Up now."

I sit back on my knees, licking my lips. I won't lie, the way he grabbed my hair was hot and it ignited the fire that I had been trying to control. Wes shakes his head once while he strokes himself. His eyes never leave my lips.

"Get on top." His husky voice commands.

Climbing up, my clit brushes over him once, instantly causing me to grind. I stop moving the minute I remember we need a condom.

"What's wrong?"

"Condom,"

He nods once and reaches over to the night-stand. The way he turns his upper body, I worry I will fall but he holds my thigh with his other hand holding me in place.

The second it's on I position him at my entrance and slowly sink down. It's pure ecstasy. That's the only way to explain how he feels inside of me.

"Fuck, Tamera." Wes growls out while gripping my ass. I swear he's going to leave marks, not that I even care right now.

We soon find the perfect rhythm, me moving up and down and him filling me over and over. I'm teetering on the edge of heaven when he brings his thumb to my clit and starts circling. I begin moving in such a frenzy that the next thing I know, I'm trembling while screaming out his name. Wes chases my orgasm with his own and then pulls me down to him. He wipes the matted hair from my sweaty face. He brings my face to his just as I feel his lips on mine. I nearly freeze. He. Is. Kissing. Me.

Wes deepens the kiss, claiming my mouth as if it is his and only his. I allow him to claim me. There's no doubt in my mind that I want this man.

When he finally lets me go, my finger goes straight to my swollen lips, tracing them. He smiles as he watches me, then slaps my ass once, causing me to let out a yelp.

"Let's go shower."

Before I can respond, he is lifting me, carrying me off to the bathroom.

It seems crazy and it's most likely a bad idea, but I think I want to get to know this side of Wes a little more.

EIGHTEEN

I'm sitting in the living room, drinking hot cocoa and chatting with Ames. We tell each other a little about ourselves. It feels right being here, like I'm home. Insane I know, but it's how I feel. There's no other way to describe it.

My phone rings from the kitchen counter, I almost chose to ignore it, but what if it is Jessy or my parents? Getting up, I see Jessy's face lighting up the screen. Why is she trying to reach me via FaceTime?

I swipe to open the chat, "Hey you,"

"Tamera, you need to come to my house, like now."

"Is everything okay, Jessy?"

She swallows and looks away from the phone

briefly. She's making me nervous. This isn't like her.

"Jessy, spill it."

"Tanner is here."

The phone falls from my hand.

Why is he here? The room starts to spin a little and I think I might be sick. I hear talking, but I can't make out what is being said, nor do I care. My ex is here, in Georgia.

"Tamera, come sit down."

Ames guides me over to a chair. Time seems to move in slow motion.

"Why is he here?"

She shrugs and holds the phone up, Tanner must now have the phone because it's his face I'm greeted with.

"Hey babe, I've missed you."

"Wha... what are you doing here, Tanner?"

"I got to thinking, and I realized I don't want to lose you. I want to make us work." I sigh at the same time Ames curses under her breath.

"Look, you should have called or texted before coming all the way here."

"I wanted to surprise you. Where are you anyway?"

"Wait, how did you know where to go?"

"I called your mom. She gave me Jessy's address."

He says it so matter of factly, like he's proud of himself. It's a little too late though. He should have done these types of things a long time ago. I throw my head back, to prevent the tears threatening.

"Don't cry babe, I'm here now."

Ha. If only he knew these tears are not for him. They are for Wes. This morning he kissed me passionately before leaving to go to the shop to check on my SUV. Now here I am not having any choice, but to leave him to go deal with my foolish ex boyfriend.

Yup, I really am going to be sick. I cover my mouth and take off for the bathroom.

I called an Uber to take me to Jessy's. Ames begged me not to go and to wait for Wes to get home. I couldn't. I was too chicken to face him. My life is a hot mess. How did it become this way so quickly? When the sun came up this morning I was wrapped in Wes's arms, now here I am face to face with Tanner. Like why?

"Babe!" He says as he pulls me in for a hug. I don't hug him back. Seeing him confirms that I made the right decision by breaking things off.

"Tanner, you need to go home."

"But I just got here and we need to fix us."

He plops down on Jessy's couch while I stay standing. No way do I want to sit next to him.

I shake my head, "There's nothing to fix. I ended things. We were going nowhere."

Seriously, he can't be that dumb that he doesn't realize this.

"I know you ended things, but I can't stop thinking about you. I want to fix this. Tell me what I need to do."

I notice Jessy in the kitchen on the phone, staring straight at me. She's whispering and I can't quite make out what she is saying. Hopefully she is chewing my mom out for giving out her address.

"Tanner, I know we spent several years together, but you had to know that I fell out of love a while ago. I'm sorry, I should have ended this a long time ago." My words are like a slap to his face. I watch as it contorts from hopeful to sad and then to anger. And for the first time in my three years with him do I start to worry.

"No, you love me Tamera. You are just being stubborn to make a point. You can drop it now. I get it."

I shake my head.

"We are going back home where we can be together. Let's go." Tanner stands, his auburn hair unkempt and not in a sexy sort of way. It looks like it hasn't been washed in days.

"Tanner," I try to reason, but his brown eyes refuse to look at me. I sigh hoping this would go a lot easier. Tanner has never been one to fight anything, unless it came to gaming.

"Dammit I said, let's go!" He shouts as he grabs my wrist and pulls me to the front door. He yanks it open with one hand while forcing me out with the other.

"Yo, who the hell do you think you are?" Jessy yells following after us. She's not one to piss off.

"Tanner, stop this!" I try to yank free, but he spins me to face him and forces me against her cabin hard. The next thing I know his lips are on mine. I don't kiss him back even though he forces his tongue in my mouth. Squeezing my eyes shut, I try to fight off him as he continues to violate my mouth. I feel bile rising and I wish more than anything, I had just stayed put at Wes's cabin. I couldn't do that to Jessy though. Clearly Tanner is crazy.

I feel arms grab me. I open my eyes just in time to see Wes deck Tanner right in the mouth which causes me to scream out in pure shock.

"Are you okay?" Jessy asks as she grabs me and pulls me back into her house. My legs feel heavy, yet somehow they move allowing her to bring me in.

"The cops are on the way."

I nod, squeezing my eyes shut while holding my chest. Tears fall hard, my mind is overcome with so many emotions. I feel myself on the verge of a breakdown.

"Oh hun, it's okay.. it's gonna be okay."

Words don't come. Just tears and I can't seem to control them as I begin to hyperventilate. Jessy just holds me until I feel shifting and several arms touching me at once, before a warm, familiar touch engulfs me.

"Tamera, look at me, you are safe now." Those masculine words cause me to snap my eyes open.

Wes.

He scoops me up and I immediately throw my arms around him. I break down all over again as his strong arms wrap around me tightly, not letting go. Life is safe in my little Wes filled bubble.

I don't know how long we stay like that. It felt like hours when in reality it was less than twenty minutes.

"Tamera," Wes whispers into my ear, "The officer is here and needs to speak to you."

Real life comes back full force and the bubble I wish I could stay in, pops.

"Ma'am, just a few questions." A female's voice states, confusing me.

I look up to see a female officer, tall, pretty.

She guides me outside where I give her a replay of what happened between Tanner and I. She jots every single word down and then repeats it all back to me.

When she is through with her questions, she hands me her card, "Here is my card, should you need anything at all or have any questions, don't hesitate to call. I'll be forwarding this case to your local sheriff's department so that they are aware of this situation should he give you any trouble once you return home," She leans in close, "but if I were you, I would pack my bags and move here. Wes is a keeper. Any girl would be stupid to leave him."

Her parting words leave me stunned while standing outside of Jessy's, in the freezing cold.

NINETEEN

Wes brings me back home to his cabin. Jessy was unsure about it at first, but finally agreed to let me leave with him. If I'm being honest, there is no place I would rather be right now. The walls of this cabin have been my safe haven the past few days. He picked me up from the side of the road when he didn't have to and allowed me to stay all through the storms. I've come to realize a real man does those things.

Ames knocks on the door before entering, a small smile on her face.

"Here, I made you some hot cocoa."

It's like she knows what I need to cheer me up. Smiling, I take it from her and take a long sip, it's soothing.

"You even put marshmallows in it."

"I did. Wes asked me to come sit with you until he comes in, I hope that's okay."

"It's fine. Thank you for being here for me."

Ames squeezes my arm, "That's what friends are for."

I laugh a little, "You hardly know me."

"Doesn't matter. I know that you are a good person and I see the way my brother looks at you. He doesn't look at anyone that way."

I continue sipping my cocoa unsure of how to respond. What does one say to that statement?

"I hope he convinces you to move here."

"Oh Ames, I don't know... "

"Ames,"

That primal voice. Just hearing him has me letting out a shaky breath.

"See," She winks and hops off the bed, shutting the door behind her.

I look at Wes and take him in. His tall build, his messy hair that peeks out from under his beanie. God it's hot. He's so hot.

"How are you feeling?"

"I'm okay, better now that you are here."

And the fact that I took a scalding hot shower when I got back. I scrubbed my body to rid Tanner's scent and scrubbed my lips harder, hating that his lips touched me uninvited.

Wes comes over to the bed and I move to

allow him more room. He pulls me to him and strokes my face gently.

"Stay with me. I know it sounds crazy, but move up here, with me."

"I.. I don't know, we don't really know each other."

"Tamera," his voice is soft, "I want you here with me. If you're really worried about us and how fast we are moving, stay at your cousin's until you are ready."

I swallow. He wants me to stay and actually move here. For him.

"What about my job?"

"You'll find a new one up here. What do you do?"

"I work in retail marketing."

"Perfect. Ames works retail, I'm sure she will be able to find you something."

I stay silent for a moment, thinking. I know sometimes I hear of people meeting someone by chance and it turns into the perfect love story, but are those real? Does that actually happen?

I'm about to find out because when he tilts my head up, I have no choice but to look at him, those sky blue eyes stare back at me. I see him opening his wounded heart up to give us a chance. A chance I think I'm going to take.

"Do you like receiving Christmas gifts?" I ask playfully.

"Yes, why?"

"Because you're about to get an early one."

He looks at me with a puzzled look.

"I'll move here."

Wes looks at me for a minute, "Really? You are going to move up here?" Excitement is crystal clear in those beautiful eyes of his now.

Pulling my bottom lip in between my teeth, I smile and nod several times like an excited child.

His fingers graze my lips, as he pulls my bottom lip free. "My lips," He murmurs before his mouth is on me. He's tender at first, kissing me slowly. It doesn't take long for it to morph into something else, it's raw, desperate almost. Wes takes my breath away. It makes me want to kiss him every single day.

As we both come up for air, he smiles, "First things first, we are going to get you a better vehicle. Can't have you breaking down.

I nudge him and together we both laugh as we get tangled up in each other, neither of us forgetting about my Christmas breakdown that led me to him.

The End.

ACKNOWLEDGMENTS

Readers~ Thank you for your love of reading.

Husband~ Thank you for putting up with my crazy Christmas obsession.

My children~ Never stop believing in your dreams, no matter how wild they may seem.

ARC Readers~ You rock! Thank you for all your support.

To my babes~ You know who you are. Thank you for reading early copies and giving me your insight. I heart you!

ABOUT THE AUTHOR

Lisamarie Kade lives in the Sunshine State with her husband, loads of children, a naked dog. Coffee and chocolate are her go to most days. She believes music is life.

When she isn't busy with her family, she enjoys reading, writing, and going to concerts.

9 798985 159905